Mannin
ning, Mick,
 and Kate visit Aunt Sue /
60

W9-ALN-934

LET'S READ WITH MAX AND KATE

Max and Kate

VISIT AUNT SUE

MICK MANNING

PowerKiDS
press™

NEW YORK

Published in 2018 by The Rosen Publishing Group, Inc.
29 East 21st Street, New York, NY 10010

"Max and Kate" by Mick Manning and illustrated by Brita Granström from *Ladybug* Magazine (October 2014)
"Max and Kate" by Mick Manning and illustrated by Brita Granström from *Ladybug* Magazine (November 2016)
"Max and Kate" by Mick Manning and illustrated by Brita Granström from *Ladybug* Magazine (January 2008)
"Max and Kate" by Mick Manning and illustrated by Brita Granström from *Ladybug* Magazine (October 2015)

Written by Mick Manning
Illustrated by Brita Granström
Compiled by Joanne Randolph

Book Design: Sarah Liddell
Editor: Joanne Randolph

Cataloging-in-Publication Data

Names: Manning, Mick.
Title: Max and Kate visit aunt Sue / Mick Manning.
Description: New York : PowerKids Press, 2018. | Series: Let's read with Max and Kate| Includes index.
Identifiers: LCCN ISBN 9781538340622 (pbk.) | ISBN 9781538340615 (library bound) | ISBN 9781538340639 (6 pack)
Subjects: LCSH: Aunts–Juvenile fiction.
Classification: LCC PZ7.M345 Ma 2018 | DDC [E]–dc23

Manufactured in the United States of America

CPSIA Compliance Information: Batch #CW18PK: For Further Information contact Rosen Publishing, New York, New York at 1-800-237-9932

CONTENTS

MAX AND KATE GO APPLE PICKING

Max, Kate, and Charlie are going to help Aunt Sue pick apples.

Max reaches up into the branches, then hands the rosy apples down to Kate.

Kate shows Charlie how to gently place them in the basket so they don't get bruised.

Aunt Sue sells the apples at
her roadside stand, along with
carrots and little pumpkins.

"The apples are selling fast!"
says Kate. "Don't worry—Charlie
and I saved the best ones for
a pie!" chuckles Max.

It's Thanksgiving! Max, Kate, and their families are visiting Aunt Sue.

Suddenly, Max points out of the patio doors. "Wow, look who else came over for breakfast!"

Everyone peeks out to see a flock
of wild turkeys. They are flapping
and pecking at tasty acorns from
Aunt Sue's oak tree.

"Big birds are dancing!" says Charlie, flapping his arms and gobbling like a turkey.

Kate and Max join Charlie's dance. Soon everyone is doing the Thanksgiving Turkey Trot!

Max and Kate are visiting his Aunt Sue's farm. "Come see what's in the barn!" she says.

14

A little lamb with a wagging tail and a woolly coat! "Baa!" bleats the little lamb. "Baa!"

Kate pets the lamb. "Oh, he's so soft and cuddly," she says.

"And noisy, too!" says Aunt Sue.
"Can you think of a good name
for him?" "How about Max?"
says Kate.

"Am I soft and cuddly?" asks Max with a grin. "No, but you sure are noisy!" chuckles Kate.

"Meet Mrs. Snuffles!" says Aunt Sue. "She's my darling Vietnamese potbellied pig."

19

Kate gives a squeal of delight
when she spots the three piglets.
"They are the cutest!" she says.

"I haven't thought of any names for them yet," says Aunt Sue. "Can you think of three good ones?"

"How about naming them after
our cuddly toys?" asks Kate.
"Mo, Kiwi, and—"

"Noo-Noo!" shouts Charlie, snuggling his elephant and pointing at the smallest piglet.

QUESTIONS TO THINK ABOUT

- What are some of the things Max and Kate do with Aunt Sue?
- What do they sell at the farm stand with Aunt Sue?
- Where do Max, Kate, and their familes go for Thanksgiving?
- What do they name Sue's animals (the lamb and the piglets)? Why?

INDEX